# CITY of SECRETS

**Victoria Ying**

Color assistant Undram Ankhbayar

VIKING

VIKING

An imprint of Penguin Random House LLC, New York

First published in the United States of America by Viking,
an imprint of Penguin Random House LLC, 2020

Visit us online at penguinrandomhouse.com

LIBRARY OF CONGRESS CATALOGING-IN-PUBLICATION DATA IS AVAILABLE
ISBN 9780593114483 (hardcover)
ISBN 9780593114490 (paperback)

Manufactured in China

10  9  8  7  6  5  4  3  2  1

THE GRAND CAPITAL CITY
OF OSKARS

Hello, who may I connect you with? Ah yes, just one moment please.

Lisa, sit up straight! No slacking today. Mr. Morgan will be here inspecting the Switchboard Operating Facility any minute!

Yes, Madame!

Madame is extra strict today. Are you alright, Lisa? You seem so tired.

I'll be okay, Anne. It's all of these rumors I've been overhearing...

I've heard them, too. War with Edmonda, our neighbors to the south.

Hey, did you bring an extra sandwich for Ever?

What a fine place you run, Madame Alexander. We are lucky to have you as headmistress of this amazing hub of communication.

Three floors and three basements, and you control it all!

Yes, I hear that the platforms and staircases all move, because this place used to be a theater. Is that true?

My, what a curious girl you have, Mr. Morgan. Should she not be better educated with a governess or at a school?

Ach, my Hannah spends every day with her governess. What's one morning out with her ol' pa? I want to show her around my new properties!

This place is amazing!

We do use the moving features of this building sometimes. For events, we often create a grand staircase.

It is a complicated facility, but I'm quite familiar with how everything works.

Must get to the lever before she tries to move the stairs!

Or else it will cause a chain reaction, and everyone will fall through the floor!

If she pulls that lever, the platform they are standing on will drop! But if I can reach that control panel . . .

I can RAISE ANOTHER PLATFORM AND NOBODY WILL GET HURT!

WHOOSH!

Oh no!

The lever also moved this catwalk!

GRAB

ROLL ROLL ROLL

WHUMP!

Hello?

Miss, you must be careful. This building is very old and some areas of it can be dangerous. Nobody knows how all of it actually works.

I thought I saw something in there . . . Something moved.

Hmmm . . . well . . . that's not quite a "something."

You heard a boy. He's an orphan named Ever Barnes. He lives here.

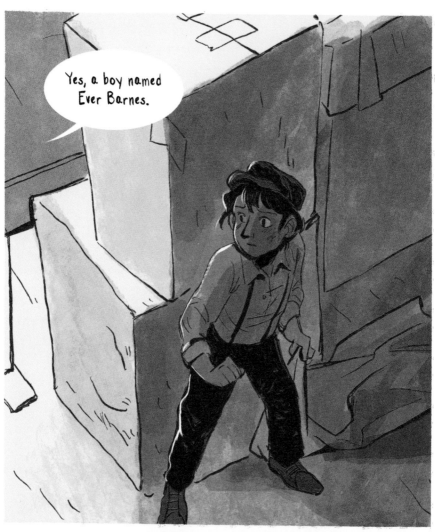

Yes, a boy named Ever Barnes.

Now, Ever, I'm going to show you the reason why we stay here.

What is it, Father?

VRRRRRRR

Whoa! The whole building is moving!

We're not done yet!

ZIPPP

What's inside of it?

The safe holds the secret. We've been lucky because we haven't had to open it, so I can't say for sure. All I know is that we must guard it and make sure it stays hidden.

Why do we need to guard it?

We do this for the good of everyone in our city. So they can be safe.

What's the secret? What are we guarding? What's keeping everyone safe?

Do you trust me?

25

Yes.

Good. I trust you too, Ever, as I trusted my father when he told me what I'm about to tell you: You know all you need to know for now.

There is more to this secret, but it's something you will learn in time, when you're a little older.

Simply protecting this very important secret and keeping this safe hidden is all you need to know now. Trust me, Ever, sometimes too much information is dangerous.

So, it's you and me protecting this secret together. Okay?

Okay.

Level 3

Madame, this car is going DOWN. The UP train is on the opposite track.

SHRUG

ding ding ding

Level Four!

Love potions! Curses! Charms! Rarities and oddities from Level Six!

A love potion! That's just what I need for Mr. Laffoon! You really CAN find anything in this market!

You don't need that! He's almost ready to propose! Besides, you know that those things aren't real.

It couldn't hurt!

Ah, you ladies must be from Level One!

No worries, ladies, I know well how to keep a secret in a city like Oskars. Speaking of secrets...

Those silly girls. Everyone knows that magic isn't real.

Ah! Madame—

DON'T speak my name. Where do you think we are?

I think if you are here, then we both already know exactly where we are.

Though, I do forget sometimes how the upper levels feel about here . . . about us. But you all still like our wares. Come inside then.

So, you say you have a pest running around in your place of employment?

I'm far from a simple employee, Cooke. I am the manager of the Switchboard Operating Facility, the communication center of the entire capital.

And I would very much like to be rid of this problem.

What type of pest are you trying to get rid of? The Baneful Hounds are not the type of animal one usually employs for things like rats.

The switchboard, eh? That's one interesting building . . . An ancient building, some would say.

A boy.

A boy?

>CLICK<

The Baneful
Hounds.

C-c-can they hunt?

You use this whistle to control them. There is only one in existence. These dogs live up to their . . . reputation.

Can they kill?

FWEE

ARF

ARF

BARK

SNARL

SCRATCH

ARF ARF! SNARK

ARF ARF

ARF! BARK! BARK! BARK!

Good.

Miss Hannah! I didn't know you were coming. I would have had Ness saddled for you.

That's alright, Greene. I'm actually looking for Jimmy.

He isn't around today. Why don't you give Ness a ride? Besides, little miss, your parents are going to wonder why your riding hasn't improved if you keep lying to them about where you're going.

I'm getting better at lots of other things, though.

Oh? Like what?

I can climb the big tree by the mausoleum in three minutes flat! That's faster than Jimmy or John!

Miss Hannah, those stable boys could lose their jobs if you keep distracting them from their work.

It's been hard 'round here, miss. I will only need one more horse groom in the next year.

. . . and the other boys will have to go find work somewhere else when they get too old to be stable boys.

Besides, you're getting older yourself. You shouldn't be out roughhousing the way you were when you were just a child.

You have lady things to do, miss.

Why does everyone keep saying that?

Because it's true.

NUZZ NUZZLE

Ness misses you, too. Why don't you go to the kitchen and see if Mrs. Byrd has an apple for her while I get her saddled for you.

Alright.

Four years ago

Father . . .

You'll see, Ever. This place, it's a hard life, but you have everything you need.

We'll look out for each other.

But I need to get home. There's something there that I have to protect—

I don't know, it just . . . felt right. Like what you'd do for a friend.

We do this for the good of everyone in our city. So they can be safe.

It's my fault he was here. It's my fault that he came after you.

I have to do the right thing, too.

The City of Edmonda

So the boy is still alive, is he?

So it seems.

This is a loose end, Cooke.

We are aware. The guild will be taking care of it . . .

Mr. President.

Hello?

Miss Hannah! What a surprise.

Hello, Madame Alexander. I've brought everyone some cookies, for being so nice to me when we visited.

...

Very well . . .

No thank you, miss.

Ah! Miss Hannah! You're back!

Hello. Lisa and Anne, right? I have something for you to say thank you for last time.

Well, isn't that sweet of you.

I thought the boy, Ever... I thought he might like one, too.

Joe? I told you, you can't call me here! I'm working!

When aren't you working, Lisa? I wouldn't ever hear my dear sister's voice if I didn't call the Switchboard.

Besides, I'm about to head to the front lines and it would be tragic if the last thing you did was call me an empty-headed ninnymuggins.

You ARE an empty-headed ninnymuggins.

Ahh, there's that warm fuzzy feeling I was looking for.

Well, there's more warm fuzzies waiting for you when you come back to us!

...

SLIP

CLICK

The dust has been disturbed.

What are you doing here?

This isn't the place for you.

But I could be your friend. You must be lonely.

I'm not and I don't want a friend.

Good thing the servants' entrance isn't locked. Mom would throw a fit.

Where have you been? What have you done to your new dress?!

It's nothing. It's just a little dirty!

FLIP

This dress was NEW from the tailor not two days ago!

I didn't want to wear it in the first place!

You never appreciate anything that your father and I do for you!

If you would just let me wear trousers—

TROUSERS? No proper girl would ever wear trousers!

Maybe I'm not a proper girl! Maybe I don't want to be one!

Hannah, you've had more broken bones than all of the boys on Level One combined.

Well?

Well, looks like you and I are in the same boat.

He's a twelve-year-old boy.

I woulda 'ad one less strike against me.

Ain't never known a man with all three eyes on the watch closed that ever saw the light of day again.

Thank ya, Batterbee, but I didn't need the reminder.

So what now? 'Cause of that boy you've got one eye closed and I've got one eye closed.

The only way to open them again is to kill 'im. Strike the fatal blow, open the eye, BAM!

But only one of us gets to do it.

So, it's a race.

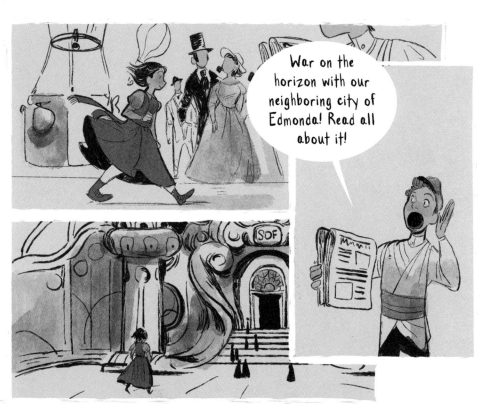

War on the horizon with our neighboring city of Edmonda! Read all about it!

Oh! Miss Hannah!

Hello, Lisa!

Looking for someone today?

Hello?

I heard you climbing.

I just wanted to see if you needed anything.

I don't.

What happened to—

SPINN

KACHOK

WHRR

WRRHR

SHOOOOP!

WHIP

Just leave me alone!

BEEP

BOOP

ZWUPPPP

VRRRRR

SWHPPP

VRRRRRP

You're hurt!

I'm fine.

Let me help you. I can—

I don't want your help. You think you want to be my friend, but trust me, you really don't. You're just going to get hurt.

Leave me alone! You're just some spoiled rich girl! I'm not just some toy that you can play with. You can't have everything that you want!

93

... fine. But someday, you might actually need someone's help.

PWOOF

Hannah?

I must find the boy . . . With his father dead . . . and Vash missing . . .

Of course!

I think he's in trouble.

Oh?

But he doesn't want my help.

Glad to be making this deal with you, Mr. Morgan. Happy to see the switchboard building go to such a generous man as yourself.

Pleased to do it. I've had my eye on this place for a long while.

Just so we're above board with everything... I should tell you, there are rumors of a young boy living here.

I've heard some rumblings.

We've done our best to cajole him, to get him to an orphanage,

but he's very resistant— and frankly very wily! Nobody has even managed to say a word to him in the past two years.

It's fine. I think I may have a solution... You can't force people to do or want things, even children.

You can't force people to do or want things, Hannah.

I guess...

The best you can do is be there for him, be ready... if he does come 'round.

YAAAAWWNN

Almost . . .
there . . .

You've cost me an eye, boy, and I got to open it!

I'm... too weak to fight back... .....

fwee fweeeee
fweeee

It's kind of poetic really . . .

The police whistle! I can't afford to get caught—

fweeeee
THUNK
fweee
fwee

fweeeee
fwee
fweeeee
fwee

How do you know how to do this?

I used to get into a lot of scrapes, falling out of trees and such. I learned how to patch myself up so my parents wouldn't find out.

I've never climbed a tree.

We should try it sometime.

This one is a favorite of mine. It's about a boy who becomes a pirate. I wish the story was about a girl pirate, though.

I wonder if those men who were after me are pirates. They sure look like them.

I'm not sure pirates like this are real.

They seemed real enough to me.

Yes sir, I'll connect you right away.

Hey, who is that man Lisa's talking to?

I don't know.

I've noticed her doing things the other girls don't do.

FWIP

I saw her with a knife once.

Lisa might be one of them.

No . . .

She might be after you. She knows you're here.

What can we do?

Lisa doesn't know that we know. We still have the advantage.

The next day . . .

Oh, Miss Hannah!

Hello, Lisa! I came by because I wanted to talk to you, about Ever.

Can you come with me?

Alright.

What is it, miss?

You can just call me Hannah.

What the—? Ever?

SWI PP !

What?

We saw you.

And I've seen you sneaking around on Level Three at night. I saw you hand envelopes to a strange man.

. . .

Who are you? Why do you want Ever dead?

SCHTICCCCKKKK

FLIP

Let's go inside and I'll tell you everything that I can.

You were right. I have been hiding something,

but I'm not trying to hurt you. I'm not with those tattooed men.

Who are they?

They belong to an assassins guild. They are known as the Bronze Knife Syndicate.

Then what are you?

... I'm a spy.

I'm a spy for our city. I'm a spy for the Oskarian government.

Why are you spying at the switchboard building?

We hear everything in the facility. I'm assigned to listen in on any suspicious communication between Edmondans and our citizens. I listen for rumblings of movement from their side. I share the information I get with other spies in our network.

Why?

Well, children, you must have heard about the coup in Edmonda. It was violent and quick. We have intelligence that says the new president there will target Oskars next.

I don't know why the Bronze Knife Syndicate wants you dead, Ever. But if you've crossed someone who then hired those assassins, then you two are going to need all the help you can get.

You want to HELP us?

If you leave anything out, I can't do anything for you.

You know my secret now. You have no reason not to trust me. You've already got a guild of assassins on your tail and I might be your only way out.

Okay. I'll tell you what I can.

I see. So these men who are after you must be after whatever is inside of the safe.

Yes, they killed my father four years ago and didn't know that I was still alive. I don't know how they found out.

Okay . . . it's good you told me, Ever. A lot is at stake.

But right now, we've got to deal with these men.

I'll speak to my contacts about them, but I want you two to lie low, keep quiet, and stay hidden. We'll talk again tomorrow and I'll have a better plan by then.

You'll be okay, Ever. You've got me and Hannah on your side now.

Yeah.

Are you alright, Lisa? You look like you haven't slept in days!

Oh, no, I'm alright, I just . . .

Is it because they deployed your brother to the front lines? I'm so sorry . . .

Yes, it's been hard. But with any luck, maybe we won't see war.

We're caretakers, Ever. A secret isn't worth anything unless we keep it from the wrong people and tell it to the right people.

How do we know who the right people are?

I hope so, Pa.

You'll know. If you have good intentions in your heart, you will find people who are like you.

I've got
some—

The code, the code to open the safe when you find it.

What?!

There's no time to explain—you have to go now! Get to that safe and open it!

That tattoo... like the one my dad had!

Gwaaaa!

137

That was the man who slashed my hand. The baker.

What? The baker is a member of the Bronze Knife Syndicate?

NOD

BANG!

CALANG!

Now to find the little rat.

You should let me get a stab at him first. He's on my miss list.

That's your business. If I find him he's mine.

Should've expected as much from you, Cooke.

GIVE ME YOUR HAT!

FWIP FWIP

I'll distract them away from you. You go find and open the safe.

143

Ah, Madame
Alexander...

How nice
to see you
again.

What are
scum like you
doing in my
Switchboard
Operating
Facility?

Well, we've
decided to provide you
with a little hands-on service
to deal with your pest
problem.

... but did I mention that its song is modeled after my own special tune?

Ah yes, I did tell you that was the only whistle in existence ...

TURN

TWEET! TWEET!

GRRRRR GRRRR GRRRR

GRRRRR GRRR

Now, allow us to conduct our business and we will be out of your hair shortly.

147

RUMBLE Rumble

SCHWINNG

!

Good work, Ever!

One, two, three to the right, one to the left.

WHIRRR

He's doing it! Vash warned us he would. He's opening the safe!

Fancy seeing you here.

"And don't pull any of the levers or mechanisms."

GRAB

SHAAAAA

FWOOOSo

There's a pattern... Something moves through here.

ARRAAHHH!!!

RRRRR

!!

I'll say, it's been a while since I danced with a lass, but it's high time we end this.

I'm out of weapons!

Aww, are ye looking pretty for me, lass?

GRAAA!

WHOOOSHHH

AAAAAHHH! WHOOOSH

KRACK

THUNK!

159

AAAARRGH!

169

171

You wretch!

KA CHUNK

RUMMM

RUMBLE

SPROIN

KRASH!

Ever! Ever, please! Tell me the code!

· · ·

EVER!!!!

Am I too late?

Ever, I don't know if you can hear me . . .

Do you hear the blue jay's call, Beyond the bright blue sea? If you can't hear the blue jay call, Then . . . we—

THRUMM mm mm
THRUMMM

Edmonda

Um, Mr. President.

There's been a development.

The Switchboard Operating Facility in Oskars . . . The caller said that "It's being opened." He said you would know what that meant.

CUNK    CUNK    CUNK

We received a phone call from Oskars.

CUNK

Thank you, Mary.

CLICK

SMASH!

They can't reveal the Megantic . . . This ends now.

Yes, Commander. I know: Launch the missile strike. Yes.

Now.

What...
what happened?

That's two
you owe me.

It's
remarkable. You
were seconds away
from suffocating,
but Hannah got
you out just in
time.

The safe. I saw it.
It's empty.

So, all of it, this, my father's murder, all of it was for nothing. Nothing at all.

Ever . . .

Ever, that's just the thing. It wasn't empty.

Drat, it's almost morning. The girls will be arriving soon.

Hannah, you show Ever the safe. I'll let them all know that the switchboard is closed for the day.

Hold on, how DID you open the safe?

This is going to sound crazy . . .

My father taught me a song when I was little. I didn't know what else to do, so I sang it to comfort you. Then the buttons on the safe started glowing.

The song was the code! Something big is happening here . . .

. . .

See?
There's nothing in here.

Ever . . .

No, wait.

No, I think it's a map of Oskars.

187

It's like a map. The switchboard building is a map of Oskars!

But why?

Well, if you can manipulate the switchboard building to hide this safe and if the building is really a map of Oskars . . .

. . . then there's another safe in the city — the safe with the REAL secret.

We need to talk to my father.

Your family lives HERE? Why in the world do you want to spend so much time where I live?

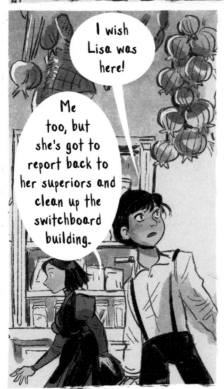

I wish Lisa was here!

Me too, but she's got to report back to her superiors and clean up the switchboard building.

Wait here.

Papa?

Ah! My dear, I'm surprised to see you at this time of day! You're usually off adventuring.

Papa, this is important.

Ever?

This is my friend.

Ever Barnes.

Ah, Ever Barnes . . .

My dear boy, you don't know how long I've waited for this moment.

We know about the safe at the switchboard building. And we're in trouble.

What kind of trouble?

With men who want to hurt Ever.

Papa, Lisa told us—

You two have uncovered far too much on your own.

This is a dangerous matter.

You should have come to me, Hannah. But there's sadly no turning back now.

I'm sorry you two have been thrust into this.

You and my father both have the same tattoos. Did you know him?

I did. More than that, I considered your father my friend.

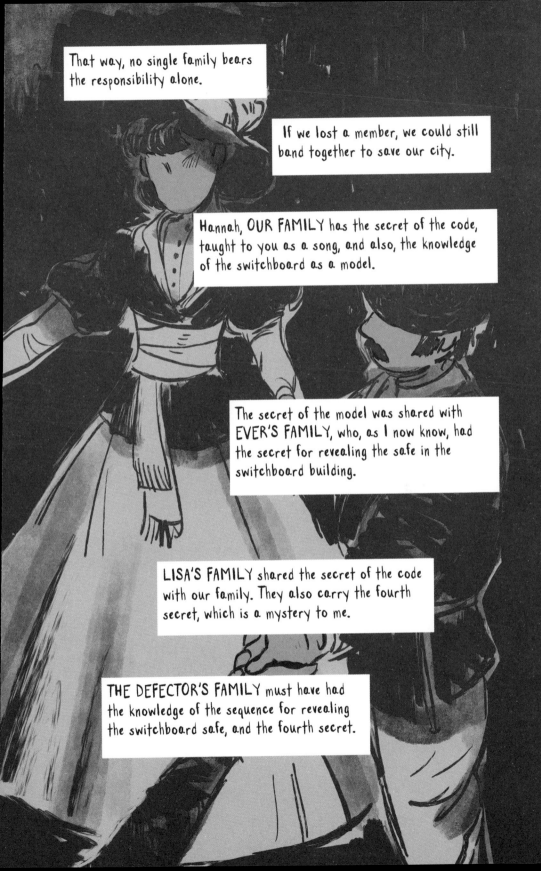

That way, no single family bears the responsibility alone.

If we lost a member, we could still band together to save our city.

Hannah, OUR FAMILY has the secret of the code, taught to you as a song, and also, the knowledge of the switchboard as a model.

The secret of the model was shared with EVER'S FAMILY, who, as I now know, had the secret for revealing the safe in the switchboard building.

LISA'S FAMILY shared the secret of the code with our family. They also carry the fourth secret, which is a mystery to me.

THE DEFECTOR'S FAMILY must have had the knowledge of the sequence for revealing the switchboard safe, and the fourth secret.

One of us did defect years ago. He disappeared and has only recently re-emerged.

He shared your father's knowledge of the sequence for the safe. When he disappeared and your father was found dead,

we believed the defector, like your father, Ever, knew the secret of the switchboard building's movable parts that reveal the safe. When your father was tragically murdered, we then thought this knowledge was lost forever.

Why did Lisa want us to open the safe?

Lisa didn't know that the real safe is in the city itself because that is not her family's secret, but she knew that you needed to work together to defeat the assassins.

So, we were right, the switchboard safe IS a map, showing us how to find the real safe.

Which we must do immediately.

Our enemies know the switchboard safe has been opened. Edmonda's missiles are aimed right at us, to stop us from uncovering any other secrets.

And there's one more thing: Our defector has recently reappeared—as the president of Edmonda!

What does the president want? What's inside the real safe that protects Oskars?

That's not one of our secrets, I don't—

FNUM MOP

PAPA!

Well,
well . . .

. . . lucky me. I
found meself another
member of the Canary
Society.

I have to get
him away from
Hannah . . .

You're fast, but you can't outrun my arrows!

Hannah!

Ever, I can't leave my father! What if . . .

We can't run away.

We have to find that other safe and save the city. I can't do it alone. Our task is bigger than both of us. Bigger than our fathers. We're responsible for everybody in Oskars.

What do we do?

We have to activate the sequence so we can find and open the real safe.

But how? The city must be ten times the size of the switchboard building.

Bigger, actually.

We'll never make it. It would take all day to reach all of the sequence activation points!

Wait.

The building . . . it's a switchboard building!

What?

It's where every citizen is connected over the phone.

Let's go, we have to get back to the Switchboard! It's our only chance!

Follow me!

The city is just a big version of the switchboard building . . .

Ready?

NOD NOD

SWOOSH

Ever! Hannah!

Lisa! The switchboard building, it's a model. The real safe is somewhere in the city! We need your help!

How can I help? Do you need the rest of the Oskarian Central Intelligence?

We need help, but not from them.

We came as soon as we heard. What do you need us to do?

Girls, this is Ever Barnes.

Hello, Ever.

Hi, Anne, thanks for all those apples.

I need you girls to listen carefully. We could stop the missiles and save the city if we work together quickly!

There's a specific sequence of events that needs to happen.

We need to call the houses at these sequence points and get them to perform a task. If we do this right, Oskar will be saved.

Okay, girls, we can do this! Abigail, call number 4372, and hand them over to Ever. Gina, I need you to call 3219.

I've got them!

Hello? Sir, yes, I know the sirens are wailing. But we can save our city. I need you to do something for me. Is there a lever in your backyard?

What? Yes, but it's broken. It doesn't do anything and we can't get rid of it!

I need you to pull that lever down three times and then up once.

And hold on—the floor below you will move!

Let's hope he believed me.

RUMBLE

RUMBLE

Lisa, I've written down all of the instructions here.

Got it.

Hannah and I have to get to the real safe!

Where's the real safe?

According to the switchboard map, the graveyard.

THoooM

221

225

SNICK

SNICK

SNICK

SNICK

We're flying!

Laser zappers?!

Incoming!

Awesome, Hannah!

Oh no! We missed one!

It's too close to the city for me to shoot it!

Um . . . sir—

It's alright. I saw.

The first Megantic has been activated . . .

Hannah! Ever! I'm so glad you're both safe!

We flew into the sky!

And we knocked all those missiles away!

I'm glad I was unconscious for most of it then!

Oh, Mama...

Hannah...

You scared me half to death!

Mama, Papa, can Ever come and live with us?

Of course he can! I searched for you, Ever, when your father died. When I couldn't find you, I thought you were gone, too. I wanted to bring you home to us then.

Really?

Of course, Ever. We want you to be part of our family.

Better hurry or you'll never catch me!

Hey! You've had more practice than me!

So, what do you think?

With all the things we've been through...

TIK

TIK

TIK